For Dimitri

DIAL BOOKS FOR YOUNG READERS
A division of Penguin Young Readers Group
Published by The Penguin Group
Penguin Group (USA) Inc., 375 Hudson Street, New York, NY 10014, U.S.A.
Penguin Group (Canada), 90 Eglinton Avenue East, Suite 700, Toronto, Ontario, Canada M4P 2Y3 (a division of Pearson Penguin Canada Inc.)
Penguin Books Ltd, 80 Strand, London WC2R 0RL, England
Penguin Ireland, 25 St. Stephen's Green, Dublin 2, Ireland (a division of Penguin Books Ltd)
Penguin Group (Australia), 250 Camberwell Road, Camberwell, Victoria 3124, Australia (a division of Pearson Australia Group Pty Ltd)
Penguin Books India Pvt Ltd, 11 Community Centre, Panchsheel Park, New Delhi - 110 017, India
Penguin Group (NZ), 67 Apollo Drive, Rosedale, Auckland 0632, New Zealand (a division of Pearson New Zealand Ltd)
Penguin Books (South Africa) (Pty) Ltd, 24 Sturdee Avenue, Rosebank, Johannesburg 2196, South Africa
Penguin Books Ltd, Registered Offices: 80 Strand, London WC2R 0RL, England

Text copyright © 2012 by Jacky Davis
Pictures copyright © 2012 by David Soman

The publisher does not have any control over and does not assume any
responsibility for author or third-party websites or their content.
Designed by Teresa Dikun and Jasmin Rubero
Text set in Aunt Mildred
Manufactured in China on acid-free paper

10 9 8 7 6 5 4 3 2 1

Library of Congress Cataloging-in-Publication Data
Soman, David.
Ladybug Girl and Bingo / by David Soman and Jacky Davis.
p.   cm.
Summary: Lulu, who likes to dress in a ladybug costume, goes camping with her parents, brother, and dog Bingo.
ISBN 978-0-8037-3582-8 (hardcover)
[1. Camping—Fiction. 2. Dogs—Fiction.] I. Davis, Jacky, date. II. Title.
PZ7.S696224Lag 2012
[E]—dc22
2011010013

Ladybug Girl and Bingo

by David Soman and Jacky Davis

Dial Books for Young Readers

an imprint of Penguin Group (USA) Inc.

"This is where we should put the tent!" says Lulu.

She's excited to be camping, and to sleep in her new sleeping bag.

"Isn't this fun, Bingo? We're going to sleep outside!"

But Bingo isn't standing by her side like he usually does.

He's zigzagging all over the campsite,

smelling everything.

Suddenly Bingo stops, puts his nose straight up in the air,

and bolts off toward the woods.

Papa quickly grabs Bingo by his collar and snaps on a leash.

"We're in the wild, not our backyard, Lulu," says Papa.

"Make sure to hold on to Bingo's leash so he doesn't get lost."

"Don't worry," says Lulu confidently. "Ladybug Girl would never let that happen!"

While her parents and brother are unpacking and pitching the tent, Ladybug Girl and Bingo decide to explore around their campsite.

The forest is filled with exciting discoveries. **Ladybug Girl** and Bingo cast spells with a **gnarly old wizard,**

ride on a galloping giant turtle,

and sip tea with the buttercup fairies
in their secret garden.

Then the whole family hikes to a nearby lake.
Bingo is pulling so hard that the leash
slips through Lulu's fingers.

Lulu's brother snatches up the leash. "I'll hold him," he says.
"You're going to let him get away."

"No I won't!" says Lulu,

taking the leash back from her brother.

When they finally arrive at the lake, they rent a canoe.
Everyone has to wear life jackets, even Bingo.
Lulu thinks that Bingo looks like a brave sea captain.

The canoe glides onto the water. Lulu loves the feeling of floating along.
When they get to the middle of the lake, her parents stop using the oars, and
they drift. It is so quiet that Lulu can hear the clouds moving. It's peaceful,
and she doesn't have to worry about Bingo running off here.

Lulu looks over the side of the canoe.

"Look!" she yells. "I see an underwater castle and mermaids!"

"That's just weeds," says her brother. Lulu looks again.

No, it's definitely a castle for mermaids and probably mer-dogs too.

Maybe her brother needs glasses.

After they return their canoe, it's time for a picnic lunch.
Lulu eats a giant cheese and tomato sandwich,
and at least thirty-eight blueberries. Bingo has two bowls of kibble.
Everything tastes better outside, thinks Lulu.

When they've finished lunch, Lulu jumps up and asks,

"Do you want to play, Bingo?" He pulls her toward the forest.

"We could play Explorers in the Jungle! How about

we're trying to find a lost unicorn, and we have to watch out for tigers?

"You stand guard right here, Bingo," Lulu says,
hooking the leash over a branch.
"And I'll climb up this tree to see
if I can find the unicorn."

CRACK!
Lulu hears the snap of a branch, and before she can blink,
Bingo is racing away, with the leash trailing behind him.
"NO, BINGO!" she yells as loud as she can. "COME BACK!!!"

"Oh no!" Lulu cries.
Where did Bingo run off to?
What if she can't find him?
What if he's gone forever?
"No!" Ladybug Girl says out loud.
She knows she will find him, even if she has to
look under every leaf in the forest.

Ladybug Girl blasts off like a rocket
to search for Bingo. She whizzes through a maze of trees,
not caring if her wings get snagged on the branches.
"BINGO!!!!!" she calls. But he doesn't come.

After she leaps over a rushing river
and stops beside a humongous boulder,
she hears a familiar snuffling sound.
Ladybug Girl zooms to the other side,
and there, rooting in circles around a pine tree, is . . .

"There you are, Bingo!" she shouts, flinging her arms around him.

"I'm so happy I found you!"

Ladybug Girl stands up and says, "Let's go back now."
She looks around, and realizes that she isn't sure how to get to their campsite.

She ran so far to find Bingo that they could be **hundreds of miles away!**
What if they need a helicopter to bring them back?

Bingo tries to climb up the big rock. **"Up here?"** asks Ladybug Girl.

Holding Bingo's leash extra-tight, she climbs to the top of the boulder.

From this high up, she can see the entire forest. She sees the Old Wizard Tree!

And then looking down she realizes she is standing on the Giant Turtle Rock!

Ladybug Girl can even see their tent.

Ladybug Girl and Bingo
run breathlessly back to the campsite.

"Mama, Papa, guess what!?
We were searching for a lost unicorn, but then Bingo escaped into the woods,
and I chased him forever. And then when I found him, we were both
lost in the woods, but then Bingo helped me figure out where we were,
and **we made it back—all by ourselves!**"

"You weren't lost," says her brother. "You were right over there. We could see your wings the whole time."

Ladybug Girl looks in the direction where they came from. It is really far away; maybe her brother doesn't need glasses after all.

Later, after dinner, they toast marshmallows around the fire.

"Can you believe we're up so late, Bingo?" Lulu asks, staring at the stars that cover the whole sky.

"Wow, there are even stars in the trees!"
Lulu says.
"Those aren't stars," her brother says,
"they're fireflies."
"Fireflies?"

"You should like them," he says.

"They're bugs that light up."

When it's time to go to sleep, Ladybug Girl wriggles into her new sleeping bag with Bingo.
"I love you, Bingo," Lulu whispers.

It has been a long day, and Ladybug Girl is a little bit sleepy, but tonight ...

Firefly Girl is up!